THE STRANGE TALE

OF THE

Snake

Ring

Matador
9 Priory Business Park,
Wistow Road, Kibworth Beauchamp,
Leicestershire. LE8 0RX
Tel: (+44) 116 279 2299
Fax: (+44) 116 279 2277
Email: books@troubador.co.uk
Web: www.troubador.co.uk/matador

ISBN 978 1784621 094

British Library Cataloguing in Publication Data.
A catalogue record for this book is available from the British Library.

Printed and bound in the UK by TJ International, Padstow, Cornwall
Typeset in 12pt Aldine401 BT Roman by Troubador Publishing Ltd, Leicester, UK

Matador is an imprint of Troubador Publishing Ltd

THE STRANGE TALE

OF THE

Snake

Ring

JOHN HOLROYD

PROLOGUE

Do you believe in magic? There's magic in this story – but not the usual kind.

No witches, no fairies, no ghosts, no horrors; but a quiet kind of magic that works gently all through the story – and you will not realise how powerful it is until the end.

If you would like to know more, turn the page and start the story…

CHAPTER 1

GERDA AND THOMAS

Long ago, in Germany, not far from the place where the River Neckar flows into the Rhine, there lived a very pretty girl named Gerda. Her parents had died when she was very small, and she had been brought up by a kind farmer, Wilhelm, and his wife Gertrud. They had looked after her with the same loving care as they bestowed on their only son, Robert.

When the story begins, Gerda was sixteen years old; she had blonde hair which she wore in two long plaits, and eyes as blue as the summer skies. As well as being beautiful, she was very happy and good-hearted, and sang as she went about her work of helping on the farm.

Now it so happened that as the farmer grew older, he was not able to work so hard or so fast on the farm, and he had recently employed a young man called Thomas, who lived in the nearby village, to help him. Thomas and Gerda often used to work together in the fields, and when they were sent to mow the hayfield by the river, Thomas would make sure that Gerda's scythe was well sharpened. He would do as many little kindnesses as he could, to make her work easier; and in return, Gerda would see that Gertrud packed him up a good helping of bread and sausage for his lunch, and that his flagon of ale was always full.

So it is not surprising that it was not long before the two young people fell in love with one another, and agreed, when they were both a little older, that they would be married.

If they had been happy young people before, they were now even happier. As she worked, Gerda made up a little song about herself and Thomas, and sang it aloud:

"I mow by the Neckar, I mow by the Rhine;
And I am so happy now Thomas is mine!"

When Thomas heard the song, he began to sing it too; but of course, he put Gerda's name in it instead of his own.

"But if we are planning to be married," said Gerda one day, "you must ask Wilhelm for his permission. It is usual for the young man to ask the girl's father. Mine, as you know, died long ago, but Wilhelm has been like a father to me, and I should be happy if you would ask him."

So that day, when they had finished their work on the farm, they went into the big warm farmhouse kitchen and both Wilhelm and Gertrud were there. Thomas explained quietly why he wished to see them, and the farmer and his wife listened intently. When he had finished, Wilhelm spoke: "Thomas, you are a very lucky young man. If you truly love one another, as you say, I would not stand between you. For many years, I had hoped that one day Gerda would marry Robert, and that you both would inherit the farm when Gertrud and I have gone; but our only wish is for your happiness."

"Robert has always been like a brother to me," said Gerda, "and I love him as a brother; but I could never marry him."

"Very well," said Gertrud, "we accept that is so, and look forward to your marriage to Thomas with great happiness. But there is another matter we must consider. We have only one farm, and that we must pass on to Robert. Although we have worked hard all our lives, we have saved little money, and have no jewellery or valuables, so you will have no dowry. And when you are married, you will have to find yourselves a house and home, as it would be unwise for two married couples to share the farmhouse."

"What shall we do, then?" asked Thomas. "I know you pay me what wages you can afford, but they are not sufficient to save money. If we have to wait until we can afford a house of our own, we shall put off our marriage for ever!"

"There is only one thing to do," replied Wilhelm. "Gerda must stay here and work on the farm a little longer while you, Thomas, go away and seek your fortune. Then, when you have enough money, come back, buy a house in the village, and marry Gerda."

Thomas said nothing. He saw his marriage and his

happiness disappearing, and was sad at the very thought of being separated from Gerda; but still he listened carefully to the rest of what Wilhelm was saying:

"I expect you've read about young men going out and seeking their fortune. Lots of them come back empty-handed. That's because they haven't any idea how to go about it. But I'm going to tell you exactly what to do. Now, tell me Thomas, who are the richest people in Germany?"

"Why, kings and queens and princes and such, I suppose," replied Thomas.

"You are quite right," said Wilhelm, "and also dukes and counts and barons and many more. And I have heard it said, that there are more kings and queens and noblemen in Germany than in any other country in the world."

"Yes, I know that such people have great wealth," said Thomas, "but how will that help me? I have often noticed that the richest people are sometimes the meanest."

"This is what you have to do," said Wilhelm. "First, you find a rich nobleman – the more important the better – and become one of his servants. At first, you must not mind how humble your tasks may be but you are a hard and cheerful worker, and soon your talents will be recognised. As you rise in the nobleman's service, you will receive higher wages; and if in the end your work becomes important to your employer, you will be able to ask any price you wish. In service, your employer provides you with food and lodging free – and so you will be able to save up nearly all your wages to come home and marry Gerda."

Before Thomas went back to his lodgings in the village that night, he and Gerda sat together on the farm gate discussing the plan that Wilhelm had suggested. Although it meant parting for a time, they both decided that it was the only answer to their problem, and neither of them could think of a better idea.

"After the haymaking is over," said Thomas, "I shall set out to find a rich nobleman who will give me work."

CHAPTER 2

THE RING

Now, after this, but before he set off on his travels, Thomas had an idea. He only had one really valuable thing in the world, a gold ring, which had belonged to his grandmother. He had promised his mother that he would never sell it, but would keep it in the family forever. This ring was like no other ring that Thomas had ever seen. It was made of the purest gold in the form of two snakes that intertwined with one another. One had red eyes made from tiny rubies, and the other had green eyes made from emeralds.

"There are many stories about the ring in our family," his mother had told him. "Some say that it can give warning of danger. Others say that if it is lost or stolen, it always returns to its rightful owner."

Thomas did not believe these stories. He thought that they were just old wives' tales.

"I shall give the ring to Gerda to keep while I am away," said Thomas to himself. "After all, when we are married she will be part of our family."

One market day Wilhelm sent Thomas into the town to sell a load of hay. When he had delivered his load, after making sure that the old mare had food and water, he went in search of a goldsmith. The goldsmith's workshop was down a narrow alley by the church.

"Good day, young fellow," said the goldsmith. "What do you wish to buy today? Or perhaps you're wanting to sell something? I give the best prices for miles around."

"I am neither buying nor selling," said Thomas, "but please look at this ring, and tell me whether you could engrave my sweetheart's name on it."

The goldsmith took the ring and examined it carefully; then he took it to the window and examined it again through his eyeglass. "What a remarkable ring!" he said at last. "In all my days I have never seen one like it. You must be a very rich young man to possess a ring like this." He paused for a moment as if in thought, then continued: "Yes, I could engrave your young lady's name; but there is little room, and it would take great skill. You are lucky that I have such skill, but it does not come cheaply. I should have to charge you a hundred crowns to do the engraving."

"You are quite wrong about my being rich," replied Thomas. "I am only a poor farm boy, and the ring is the only valuable thing that I possess. I could not possibly pay you a hundred crowns. Give me back my ring, and I will not trouble you any further."

"Wait a moment," said the goldsmith. "I have an idea. If you would allow me to take one of the jewels from the eyes of the snakes, I would accept that as payment."

"I cannot agree to that," answered Thomas. "I cannot give a ring with a jewel missing."

"Well," said the goldsmith, "there is just one more way, but if you do not agree to this, I cannot help you. Will you allow me to shorten and flatten each of the snakes' tails. Then I could engrave your name on one, and your sweetheart's name on the other. In doing this I would remove a small quantity of gold. The ring is of such high quality that it would pay me for my work."

"I agree," said Thomas. "Our names are Thomas and Gerda."

"Leave me the ring," said the goldsmith, "and come back in two hours."

Later that day, as Thomas drove the mare back to the farm, he was contented with his day's work, and resolved not to delay any longer than necessary before setting out on his travels.

A few days later, the haymaking was finished, and the hay safely stacked in the barnyard. In the evening Thomas went in again to see Wilhelm and Gertrud.

"My good friends," he said, "at daybreak tomorrow I must be on my way. Thank you for all that you have done for me, and for your valuable advice. I have no doubt that you will keep Gerda safe until I return, and as you have cared for her since she was a baby, it will be no hardship for you to do so for a little longer. I give you my word that I will return the very moment that I am able to marry her."

"Goodbye, my boy," said Wilhelm, and shook

Thomas's hand warmly. Gertrud embraced him, and a tear trickled down her cheek.

There was even more sadness at parting with Gerda; but the brightness came back into her eyes when she saw the ring, which Thomas produced from his pocket.

"Take this ring," said Thomas, "and keep it safe until I return. Look! Both our names are engraved on it; and every time you look at it, it will remind you that I promise to come back to marry you, and then we shall be together for always."

So Gerda dried her tears, and they said their final farewells at the farm gate.

"I will keep the ring on my finger always," said Gerda quietly, "and every evening I shall wait here at the gate for a while, and look up the road to see if you are coming home."

And so Thomas returned to his lodgings in the village, where he packed his few belongings in his knapsack. After a frugal supper, he lay down on his bed to sleep. But he was both sad and excited at the same time, and this state of mind made it impossible for him to sleep. When the first glimmer of light entered his window, he was still wide awake, thinking of happy days with Gerda in the past, the pain of parting, and wondering what the future held for both of them. Now the first ray of sunshine was peeping in. Thomas dressed himself, and put on a strong pair of boots. He added a loaf and a large piece of cheese to the contents of his knapsack, filled his water bottle from the well, and stuck his knife into his belt. Finally, taking a stout staff in his hand, he closed the door behind him and set off down the dusty road, with scarcely a glance behind him.

CHAPTER 3

THE PECULIAR PRINCE

Thomas walked briskly on until the sun grew hot at noon. Then he rested in the shade of a tree, ate a little of his food, and refreshed himself with a drink. When it grew a little cooler, he walked on. As the sun was setting he came to a farm. The farmer was just taking a last look at his animals before going indoors for his supper.

"May I sleep in your barn tonight?" asked Thomas politely. "I am on a journey and I shall be gone by morning."

"Yes, certainly," replied the farmer. "The hay is soft and dry, and you may help yourself to a drink of cider from the barrel."

Early next morning he was on his way again. He walked on again for the whole of the second day, and that night slept in a dry ditch.

His third day's march took him through a gloomy forest, where the trees were so close together that there was hardly a glimpse of the sky. From time to time he kept thinking that someone was following him, as he heard rustlings in the undergrowth; but he saw no one, and decided that the sounds were made by woodland creatures. He walked cheerfully on his way, but he would not have been so cheerful if he had known what the sounds really were. For in the wood lived two robbers, who would wait for rich travellers to pass through the forest, and would pounce on them and relieve them of their money and valuables.

Thomas learned later that they were known as Riese and Zwerg. These names mean Giant and Dwarf, because one was an enormous man of great strength, and the other very small and wiry. In fact, before they took to being robbers in the forest, they had both worked in a travelling show. Riese was the strong man, and Zwerg an acrobat and tightrope walker.

Fortunately for Thomas they took a good look at him from the shelter of the trees. He seemed to them to be a poor traveller not worth the trouble of robbing, so they allowed him to go peacefully on his way.

As the sun set Thomas emerged from the forest and looked for somewhere to spend the night. He ate the last few morsels of his bread and cheese, and found a clear spring of water to have a drink and refill his water bottle. A little further down the valley was a hay field, and settling down in a swathe of hay that had been raked up to dry, in a few moments was fast asleep.

When he awoke the next morning to begin the fourth day of his journey, he was cold and hungry. But he set off with a will, and soon he could see in the distance a town on the top of a hill. At the very summit there was a castle.

"Rich noblemen live in castles," said Thomas to himself. "If I step out briskly, I should be there by mid-day."

But it was further away than he thought, for it was not until sunset that he came to the walls of the town. At the gate, a soldier was on guard.

"Halt!" cried the soldier, "and hear what I have to say! No rogues, vagabonds, pedlars, highwaymen or minstrels are welcome here, by order of the prince. So if you are any of those things, please be on your way to some other town."

"I am none of those things," replied Thomas, "I am an honest man looking for work, and if you will let me in, I intend to seek your prince, who I suppose lives in the castle on the hill, to ask if he has any employment for me."

"You are right in thinking that he lives in the castle," said the soldier, "but I have my reasons for thinking that he will not employ you. More than that, I dare not say. But there's no harm in trying: so enter in peace."

So Thomas strode through the gate, and began to climb a steep, cobbled street. He thought, quite correctly, that if he kept climbing, he would reach the castle in the end. Halfway up the street he stopped to take his breath, and as he did so, he noticed a beggar sitting on a doorstep with a small wooden bowl on his lap.

"Kind young gentleman," called the beggar in a

whining voice, "spare a few coins for a poor old man, wounded in the French wars, no friends or relations – just a few pennies would do."

This was the dirtiest, raggedest beggar that he had ever seen, and Thomas felt quite sorry for him. Reaching into his pocket he found a few small coins and dropped them into the begging bowl.

"Thank you kindly, young gentleman," said the beggar, "but surely you are a stranger here – what might your business here be?"

"I am looking for work," replied Thomas, "and I very much wish to work for the nobleman who owns the castle on the hill."

"He is the Prince of Schwarzburg," said the beggar. "I have never set eyes on him, that is, so far as I know. But it is said that he puts on various disguises, and walks about the town listening to what the people are saying about him. If he hears someone speaking disrespectfully, that person will find himself arrested and thrown into a dungeon."

Now Thomas had never heard of a prince who did such a thing, and thought it quite a shabby trick for the prince to play on the townspeople. He could not help exclaiming, in quite a loud voice, "What a peculiar prince!"

"Hush!" cried the beggar, "do not say such things. The prince himself might be hiding in yonder doorway or round the next corner. You should not even say such things to me, as it's said that he sometimes disguises himself as a beggar."

"Thank you for warning me!" said Thomas, and looked in the doorway and round the corner, but there was no one in sight except an old woman sweeping the doorstep of the house opposite. He said goodbye to the beggar and set off again up the steep hill to the castle. When he explained to the sentry at the gate that he was looking for work, he was directed to the door of the castle kitchens. The chief cook was a fat, jolly man who invited Thomas into the kitchen.

"Looking for work, are you?" asked the cook. "Well, the only work I have is washing the dishes, but I suppose that a bright young man like you might be too proud to do work like that!"

"I'm not at all proud," said Thomas, "and I will do any work you ask."

"Very well," said the cook. "You are hired as third dishwasher. Now go and wash yourself at the pump in the yard, and come back here. I'll find you some leftovers to eat, and you can start work straight away."

The leftovers turned out to be a large piece of game pie, several pieces of bread and a small mug of beer. Thomas was so hungry that this seemed to him like a wonderful banquet. He congratulated himself on his good fortune, and did not mind working as hard as he could, washing what seemed like a mountain of dirty vegetable pans and dishes. At last all was finished, and the two other boys who were the first and second dishwashers showed Thomas the small attic room, furnished with three narrow beds.

"Our beds are hard and not very comfortable," said one of the other boys.

"When you have been sleeping on the ground any bed is better than none," answered Thomas.

He stretched out as comfortably as he could and was soon fast asleep.

Next morning Thomas and his two companions were up at dawn, and were soon in the kitchen washing the first of the day's dirty dishes.

"Now, listen to me you three," said the cook, looking rather worried. "I have just heard that the prince is coming to inspect the kitchens this morning. When he arrives, do not stop work until you are told. Do not say a word unless the prince addresses you, which is unlikely. But if he should happen to do so, bow, answer politely, and call him 'Your Highness'."

The boys went on with their work, and sure enough, later in the morning, the prince strode into the kitchen, followed by his steward and two soldiers with drawn swords. Thomas continued to wash dishes, as he had been told. The prince walked all around the kitchen, the dairy, the stillroom and the larder, and every now and then muttered something to the steward. Just as everyone thought that he was about to leave, the prince moved to where Thomas was working, and stood a few paces behind him.

"Turn round, boy, and face me," snapped the prince.

Thomas did so.

"Are you new here?"

Thomas bowed politely. "Yes, Your Highness."

"Where do you come from?"

"From a village south of the forest, Your Highness."

"I KNOW WHO YOU ARE!" shouted the prince angrily. "YOU ARE THE PERSON WHO WAS TALKING ABOUT ME IN THE STREET. YOU CRIED OUT LOUDLY THAT I AM PECULIAR!"

Thomas was too startled to reply.

"To the dungeon with him!" ordered the prince.

One of the soldiers sheathed his sword, produced a length of chain from his belt, and secured Thomas's hands. Then the other soldier joined in and between them they half pushed and half dragged him out of the kitchen, down a flight of stone steps and into a small, dark underground cell. The heavy door shut with a clang, and the key was turned in the lock.

There was a small, square hole at the top of the door, and by the small amount of light that filtered through, Thomas could just make out the details of his prison. It was just a small bare cell furnished only with a wooden box to sit on, and a heap of straw in one corner. That day went by more slowly than any day that Thomas could remember. At noon a soldier brought in a mug of thin soup and a piece of dry bread.

In the afternoon he sat on the box and thought about his situation.

"Well," he said to himself, "that will teach me a lesson: that it is not always wise to say aloud what you are thinking. That old woman sweeping the steps must have been the prince in disguise. But what can I do now?"

But no matter how hard he thought, he could not see any way out. He tried the door to make sure it was firmly locked. He felt all round the walls but found nothing but smooth stone. There was nothing to do but make the best of it. When night came he curled up on the straw. *At least I'm used to sleeping rough, so I shall probably have a good night's sleep*, he thought.

But he was mistaken. There was very little straw, and the stone floor was hard and cold. He was still awake when, in the early hours of the next morning, Thomas saw a glimmer of light coming from the door. Then he heard the key turn in the lock, the door was opened, and there stood the cook in his shift and nightcap, with a candle in one hand and Thomas's knapsack in the other.

Before Thomas could say anything, the cook began: "The prince said I could let you out as soon as it was morning. When the soldiers had taken you away, he turned to me and said that you couldn't be all bad because you had given some coins to a beggar, but you had to be taught a lesson so you could stay in the cell till this morning."

Thomas nearly said, "What a peculiar prince!" but remembered in time, and instead said: "What a kind prince!"

"Mind you," continued the cook, "he's just as likely to change his mind again as soon as he is awake; so I advise you to leave here as quickly as you can, and be well away from the town before it's light. Now, I've put your belongings, some food and your water bottle in your knapsack – so take it, and good luck to you."

"Thank you very much indeed," said Thomas. "You are the kindest man I've met since I left home."

"Go out through the kitchen and to the main gate. When you come to the sentry, say to him, 'Open the gate, in the prince's name!' – and he will open it. When you get to the market cross, turn westwards, and in that direction there is a small wicket gate with no guards. Once again, goodbye, and good luck."

Thomas followed the cook's instructions, and by the time the sun rose, he had left the peculiar prince's kingdom far behind.

CHAPTER 4

THOMAS TRAVELS ON

Now followed many days of travelling. The weather became hotter, and the roads drier and more dusty, but Thomas travelled steadily on. Every few days it was necessary to stop and ask for work at some farm or orchard, but this was only to earn a little money for food, which would keep him alive during the next stage of this journey.

Once or twice he came to a great mansion or to a castle, where he tried to be taken into the service of the lord, but he had no success.

"There's plenty of work to be had on the farms and in the vineyards," said the steward at one enormous house, and that seemed to be the general opinion. So Thomas had, for the present, to content himself with farm work. As the summer wore on, some of the farms began the corn harvest. When that was gathered in, there was the grape harvest in the vineyards that sloped steeply down the hillsides to the great River Rhine. As usual, Thomas worked hard, and his cheerful nature made him popular with the farmers and with the other workers.

But at last the grapes, too, were all gathered in. Thomas thought that it was time to set off again to search for a nobleman who would employ him, and thus make it possible to carry out his plan to return and marry Gerda. But just at that time, the weather changed for the worse.

Instead of day after day of warm sunshine, there was cold, drenching rain, blown along by gale force winds, which swept across the countryside.

This weather lasted for several weeks, and when it eventually stopped, the roads were almost knee-deep in mud. Even men on horseback were not able to travel far. The farmer who owned the vineyard where Thomas had been working, whose name was Franz, said to him:

"Thomas, I know you are wishing to be on your way, but you are very welcome to work here for the winter. There are lots of jobs to do indoors."

"Thank you very much," replied Thomas, "but I have told you my story, and you realise why I must go as soon as I can."

"Listen to me," said Franz seriously, "I know the weather in these parts much better than you do. When this rain has passed by, the wind will turn into the east. There will be night after night of snow, until it lies deep on all the hills. The river will run so fast and deep that it is dangerous to take out a boat. In fact, it is almost impossible to travel until the snows melt in the spring. Better to stay here than to be found frozen to death in the hills!"

All the other workers on the farm told him the same story, and begged him, if he valued his life, to remain safe and warm on the farm until the winter had passed. Thomas agreed. Franz paid him well and gave him excellent food and lodging, and Thomas was even able to save a little money from his wages. The winter soon passed by, and Thomas was happy and comfortable in his work on the farm.

Spring came, and the outdoor work began, but Thomas did not set off on his journey again. Franz thought to himself: *Perhaps he has forgotten his sweetheart at home, and he will be content to stay here and work for me. He is such a good worker that I should be sorry to lose him.*

But when haymaking season came round, the sweet smell of the new mown hay, and the sound of the stone on the scythe, reminded Thomas of home, and of mowing the hay by the river with Gerda. He even remembered the little song, which they had sung together. Then he began to feel guilty that he had stayed with Franz so long.

Once he had made up his mind to continue his journey, he sought out Franz, and said to him, "Franz, you are a good friend as well as a good master. So much so, that I have stayed too long with you, when I should have been on my way. But now my thoughts are all on my home and my sweetheart, so I must go at once."

"I am very sorry to see you go," replied Franz, "but go with my blessing and a piece of advice: travel north until you come to the Kingdom of the Shining Sea.

Everyone says that the king of that country is the richest and most generous nobleman in the whole of Germany."

So early the next morning, Thomas set out on his travels once more. The weather had turned fine and warm, and travelling was pleasant in that part of the country. Nevertheless, it was a very long way to the Shining Sea, and it was several more weeks before Thomas, tired and footsore, arrived at the palace of the king. By now he knew that the kitchen was the place where it was possible to obtain employment, but when he arrived at the kitchen door, there were already about twenty men and boys of different ages lining up outside.

"Get to the back of the queue!" called several of them. "If there's any work going, it's first come, first served here," said one.

The door opened and a tall man in a chef's hat and white apron stepped out. "I'm the head cook," he announced, "and I can tell you that there is a job for only one man today." The man at the head of the queue stepped forward.

"Have you ever worked in a nobleman's kitchen before?" the chef asked him.

"No, I haven't," replied the man.

"You are no good then," said the chef. "The king told me only to employ men with experience. Have any of you others ever worked in a nobleman's kitchen?" No one answered. The chef turned and was just about to disappear into the kitchen again, when Thomas suddenly remembered his experience with the 'Peculiar Prince'.

"Yes! I have worked for the Prince of Schwarzburg," cried Thomas loudly. He thought it wise not to mention that he had only worked there for a few hours.

The chef turned back, and said to Thomas, "In that case, you are just the man I want. Congratulations! You have just been appointed dishwasher to the king. Come with me, and as for you others, off you go as quickly as possible. You can see that this young man has been given the appointment."

The chef led the way into the kitchen, and Thomas followed.

CHAPTER 5

GERDA IN DESPAIR

Gerda missed Thomas very much. She went about her work on the farm very much as before, but she rarely sang at her work as she had done in the past. When she did, her little song had changed, and the words were now like this:

"I once had a sweetheart, but now I have none;
And I'm so unhappy now Thomas has gone."

Every day after her work was done, she waited for a while at the gate, but no one ever came. The weeks and months went by. Winter came and spring, and then haymaking season came round again.

One day Gerda had been sent alone to begin mowing the field by the river. It was hard work, as she could never get her scythe as sharp as Thomas used to make it. After a while she tried to lighten the work by singing, but found that the words had changed again:

"What use is a scythe that's too blunt to cut hay?
What use is a sweetheart who is so far away?"

As soon as she had sung the last line, she was sorry, and thought to herself, *I should not sing words like that, as I expect Thomas is working very hard to make enough money to come home and marry me.* And she was so unhappy that she stopped her work, sat down on the riverbank and began to cry. To comfort herself, when she had rubbed the tears from her eyes, she took off the ring that Thomas had given her, and pressed it between her hands.

But her fingers were wet with her tears, and the next moment she had dropped the ring, which rolled down the steep bank into the water. Immediately Gerda stooped down and stared into the water. The river ran deep by the bank, and all she could see in the depths was a large fish, which flicked its tail and disappeared into the middle of the stream.

Although Gerda had lived by the river all her life, she had never learned to swim and dare not trust herself to the swirling water. So she sought out Wilhelm, who was working on another part of the farm. With tears still streaming down her cheeks, she told him what had happened. He quickly called Robert, and the three of them returned, with nets on long poles, to where the ring had disappeared. They spent a long time dredging the bottom of the river with the nets, but without success. In the end Robert stripped and dived repeatedly into the water, but found nothing.

"Either the current has carried it away," he said, "or it has sunk too deeply into the mud to be found." What none of them realised was that the brightness of the ring as it entered the water had attracted a fish, which had immediately swallowed it.

This was the selfsame fish that Gerda had seen swimming away when she first looked into the water.

When Robert had returned to the farm to dry himself, Gerda turned to Wilhelm, and said sadly, "This is the worst day of my life. What shall I do? How am I to tell Thomas when he returns that I have lost the ring? It was the only valuable thing he possessed, and he gave it to me to keep forever!"

"You must be in despair," answered Wilhelm, "but you must remember that you are much more precious than any ring, no matter how valuable. I am sure that Thomas will think so too."

Gerda knew that Wilhelm was right, and that Thomas would value her more highly than any possession; but from now on she was torn between a longing for his return, and fear of his discovery that the ring was lost.

Many times she stood in the place where the ring had disappeared, hoping that one day the water would be clear enough for the ring to be seen at the bottom of the river. But of course, it was nowhere to be found.

Then, three months later, a letter from Thomas arrived. Now in those days, it was both difficult and expensive to send letters. They could take weeks or even months to be delivered, and sometimes they never arrived at all. Also, not many people could read and write, and it was fortunate that both Gerda and Thomas had been taught to do so when they were children, by the nuns at a nearby convent. The letter consisted of a piece of parchment rolled up, and sealed with a piece of red sealing wax. The letter read as follows:

Written from the king's palace.

My dearest Gerda,

I miss you very much and I long to be home with you.

I have good news. After a long and weary journey I arrived at the king's palace, where I was given work in the kitchen. I have already been promoted from washing dishes to waiting on the king's table. I have a smart new uniform and get good food from the kitchen. I have already started saving my wages. There is a very important man in the palace called the Lord Chancellor who has been very kind to me. I do not know why, because he has a much higher position than I have, only a little below the king and the queen. One day I told him about you, and he gave me this piece of parchment to write on, and showed me how to send a letter. I've nearly filled it now, so keep on watching and waiting for me, and think of me every day when you look at your ring. As soon as I have saved enough I shall be on my way home. Give my love to everyone at the farm. And very much love to you, especially to you,

from your Thomas.

A tear trickled down Gerda's cheek as she read the words about the ring. She was still very depressed by the loss of it, but after reading the letter several times, she felt a little better. "I must not mope about, as I have been doing," she said to herself. "Thomas is working so hard for me, and saving his wages. Some young men, if they were far away, would spend all their money on themselves. So I must be brave, and as soon as he comes home I must own up about the ring and hope that he will forgive me."

CHAPTER 6

THE KING'S FEAST

The weeks rolled by at the king's palace, and now it was spring again – two years after Thomas left the farm. By this time he was well liked by both the king and the chancellor. Each mealtime he stood behind the king's chair and attended to his needs, and sometimes the king even asked him to taste a little of the royal food, to see whether it was properly cooked.

Sometimes the queen sent for him to attend her in the royal chambers, where he was asked to tell a bedtime story to the two little princesses. By now he was quite well paid, and was able to put away money each week towards the time when he would have saved enough to buy a house and marry Gerda.

Now each year, at the time called Lent, which comes just before Easter, it was the custom for the king to give a banquet for the learned professors from the nearby university. There were seventeen of them, all very old and wise. The king found it very difficult to talk with them through the meal, because it was not considered polite for anyone but the king to begin a conversation. The professors were not interested in the weather, or his family, or how good the hunting was this year, or any of the other things that the king normally talked about.

He usually solved the problem by asking them a question that he thought they could not answer, and by the time each one of them had tried to answer it, the meal would be over. This year he had decided to ask: "What holds up the world?" and thought their answers would take at least an hour.

The day before the banquet was to take place, the king sent for the head cook. "Tomorrow is the professors' feast," he announced, "and as usual in Lent, we eat no meat; so the main course will be fish."

"Certainly, Your Majesty," replied the cook.

"Now listen carefully," continued the king. "The last time you served fish at one of my banquets, you cut it into pieces and smothered it with sauce so that I couldn't tell whether it was salmon or stockfish. So this year, I want one fish, big enough for nineteen people. Cook it whole and serve it on your biggest dish. And if you make sauce, serve it separately."

"Very well, Your Majesty," said the cook; and he bowed and returned to the kitchen.

The next day at the appointed time all the professors arrived for dinner. The king and queen sat in their usual places at the head of the table, and the professors in order of age round the rest of the table, the oldest next to the king. Thomas stood in his usual place behind the king's chair, ready to carry out any task that the king ordered. Other servants were hurrying round, serving everyone with bowls of steaming onion soup.

No one spoke, as they were all waiting for the king to ask his question. After he had taken a spoonful of soup, as a signal that the others could begin, he asked in a loud voice: "What holds up the world?"

"Atlas, the son of Lapetus, holds up the world, Your Majesty," said the oldest professor.

"Then who holds up Atlas?" asked the king.

"He stands on the back of a giant turtle," said the second oldest professor.

"And what holds up the turtle?" enquired the king.

"It rests on the back of an enormous elephant," answered the third professor.

"And the elephant," continued the fourth, "stands with its legs firmly in the waters that are beneath the earth, which were divided on the second day of creation."

No one else spoke. After a few minutes' silence, the king asked, "Do you all agree on that?"

"Yes. Yes, we do, certainly, quite true, quite true," said all the professors together.

Silence again.

This is going to be quite embarrassing, thought the King. *What can I ask them now?*

Fortunately there was an interval filled with the clatter of bowls and spoons as the servants collected the soup plates. The head cook appeared in shining white hat and apron, carrying an enormous oval dish, on which had been cooked the largest fish Thomas had ever seen.

"What a wonderful fish!" cried the king. "Thomas, give my congratulations to the cook, and tell him to pass them on to the fisherman who caught it! It's a fish fit for a king – so much so, that I shall serve it out myself."

So the king took a sharp knife, slit the great fish in two, and opened it. As he did so, he was amazed to see the gleam of gold and the flash of jewels from the fish's inside. In a moment, with the point of his knife, he had recovered from the fish's belly – a ring! He held it up for everyone to see.

"Look, gentlemen, what I have found inside the fish," he exclaimed. "A ring, the like of which I have never seen before. I have many rings in my treasury, but none like this."

As he said that, a wonderful idea came into his mind – another question he could ask the professors, that would keep them talking until the end of the meal.

Telling the servants to carry on quietly with the serving of the fish, he turned to the professors. "I am going to ask you learned gentlemen another question, and perhaps you can help me to find the correct answer. The question is, who is the rightful owner of the ring – because it is clearly very valuable?"

No one answered.

So the king continued: "Is it mine, because the fish was bought with my money? But I paid for a fish, not a precious ring. Does it belong to the fisherman? Well, he didn't ever know it was there, or he would have kept it for himself, or sold it to me for a good price. Or does it belong to the person who owned it before it got inside the fish? If so, who could that be?"

Again, there was silence.

"Come, come, gentlemen!" exclaimed the king. "One of you must have some idea."

"Your pardon, Your Majesty," ventured the oldest professor, "but we do not know. There is no way of finding the right answer to your question."

The king could hardly believe that none of the professors could give an opinion. "Look," he said in the end, "I will give a bag of gold to anyone in this hall who can give me the answer."

Another embarrassing silence.

Just then a small voice from behind the king's chair said, "Please, Your Majesty, may I speak?" It was Thomas.

"Yes, Thomas you may. I suppose you can solve the puzzle when the learned professors have failed?" He smiled, while the professors began to laugh and chatter between themselves.

"Silence!" barked the king. "Let the boy speak."

"Please, Your Majesty," began Thomas, "with respect, the ring does not belong to you. Neither does it belong to the fisherman. The ring is mine."

There were gasps of surprise. Then the king spoke again: "How can that be? How could it be yours?"

"If Your Majesty will look again at the ring, you will see that it is made from two snakes with jewels for eyes. And if you will look carefully at the tails, you will see how my name has been engraved on one, and that of my sweetheart Gerda, on the other. There is no other ring like this in the whole world."

The king looked carefully. "It is just as he says: the names of Thomas and Gerda are written here. Thomas, take your ring and after supper come to my private chamber and we will talk about your reward."

CHAPTER 7

THE KING MAKES
AN OFFER

When the banquet was over, the professors returned safely to their lodgings in the university. Thomas made his way to the king's chambers. He was in a confused state of mind regarding Gerda: a little cross, perhaps, that she had not kept the ring safely.

"Perhaps she sold it," he said to himself. "In which case, either she is in trouble and needed money, or she doesn't care about me any more. Or perhaps she lost it. If so, she will be very upset about what I shall say to her when I get home."

As he arrived at the king's door he was just saying to himself: "If the king keeps his promise and gives me a bag of gold, I must set off at once and go back home and if he doesn't…

"Come in, come in, my boy," said the king in a friendly manner as Thomas arrived at the door of his chamber. "Sit down here." He pointed to a stool, which was beside his feet. Thomas sat rather uncomfortably on the edge of the stool.

"Here is your bag of gold which I promised," continued the king. "I believe what you said about the ring, that it belongs to you and your sweetheart, Gerda. I wish you to tell me about this girl, and about your home."

"She is very beautiful, and also kind and loving, Your Majesty," replied Thomas, "and she lives on the farm where I used to work before I set out on my travels. Before I left, I gave her the ring, and promised that I would make my fortune and return and marry her."

"Now, listen to me, my boy," said the king. "I think you can do better than go home and marry a farm girl, no matter how beautiful. Surely you prefer a palace like this to a farm!"

Before Thomas could reply, the king continued: "Now, the Lord Chancellor and I have watched you carefully ever since you came into my service. Even the most menial tasks you have carried out cheerfully and thoroughly, without ever a complaint. You have been honest and truthful. In fact, I think you might be the boy I have been seeking: to carry out a difficult and noble task, with great responsibilities but great rewards. You see, I have no son, so I am seeking a young man who could be trained to be king when I die."

Thomas was so amazed at this speech that for a moment he could say nothing. Then at last he managed to stammer, "B-but Your Majesty, surely your people would not accept one of your servants as king?"

"By then," replied the king, "you would be the greatest in the land. First, I would make you a knight. You would learn horsemanship and warrior's arts, and be addressed as Sir Thomas."

Then in a year or so, you would become vice-chancellor, and after that, a lord. After a few years, you would marry one of the princesses – they both think the world of you already – so of course, you would have to be made a prince. All this time you would be learning about politics and the history of the kingdom, so you would have the knowledge to become a wise and well-loved king."

Thomas was silent. After a while, he said quietly, "But Your Majesty, I have made a promise to Gerda."

"Young people often make promises," replied the king, "that life makes it impossible for them to keep. Gerda is young; if she is kind and beautiful she will soon find someone else to marry. Besides, she has either lost your ring, or sold it, so she cannot be as faithful as you may think."

Thomas wished to deny all this, but he thought it rude to contradict the king directly. While he hesitated, the king continued: "Don't answer me now. Go to your room, think about my offer, and sleep on it, and I will send for you in the morning."

As Thomas rose from the stool, and turned to go, the king added: "You must decide, only you, so do not speak to anyone about this. And if you decide to leave, you shall have a horse to ride, and fine clothes, as well as the gold, so that you can return home in comfort."

Thomas returned to his room and lay on his bed. The king's words were still ringing in his ears: "You would be the greatest in the land."

Perhaps he could accept the king's offer and still marry Gerda. *If I can be made into a prince*, he thought, *then surely someone so good and beautiful as Gerda could be made into a princess.* But it did not take him long to realise that it would be very difficult for the people of the kingdom to accept him as king, if he did not marry the eldest princess. Then he thought how he could help Gerda to bear the disappointment if he never returned to the farm. If he were king, he could send her money and fine clothes, even find a rich nobleman to be her husband.

He fell into a long daydream about the pleasures of being a king. He could, he thought, do as he pleased in every way. There would be banquets, and dances, and entertainments of all kinds. There would be hunting the wild boar in the forests, and rewarding the winning knights in tournaments of jousting...

"Thomas! Thomas! Are you there?" Thomas was surprised by a voice calling his name, and a quiet, timid knock. He awoke from his daydream and opened his door. There stood the elder of the two young princesses. She had wrapped herself in a large shawl, which must have belonged to the queen.

"I'm not really allowed in this part of the palace," said Princess Rosa in an urgent whisper, "but I had to come and talk to you. I heard my father saying that you might be leaving, so I came to ask you to stay. Please stay, we shall miss you so much. Please promise me you'll stay."

"I'm sorry, Your Highness, but I can't make a promise that I may not be able to keep," answered Thomas. "In many ways I want to stay, in other ways I feel I must go. But I promise to think very carefully about it. Now you must go, or we shall both be in trouble. The king ordered me not to speak to anyone about it."

The princess gathered her shawl more tightly around her, and without another word hurried away down the long echoing corridor towards the royal apartments.

Thomas lay down once again on his bed. The princess's visit had made it even harder to decide what to do. He had become very fond of both Rosa and her younger sister, and it would be hard to say goodbye to the two girls for ever.

His daydream had passed, and would not return, no matter how hard he tried to recapture it. Instead of passing quietly into sleep, he tossed and turned on his bed while his thoughts became ever more confused and difficult. At last he fell into a deep but troubled sleep.

In his dream, it seemed as though he was a young boy again. He was in the convent near his home, where kind Sister Agnes had taught him to read, in exchange for weeding the vegetable garden and feeding the carp in the convent fishponds. He seemed to be sitting on a stool by the nun's side, looking at the book, which lay open on her lap. He could see the great decorated letter at the head of the page, but could not make out any of the writing. But he could hear the sister's voice, saying softly but very clearly, "Remember, Thomas! Beware the kingdoms of this world, Thomas, and all their glory!"

Thomas awoke with a start. It was quite dark, and he was shivering. He covered himself with his blankets and fell into a deep and dreamless sleep.

CHAPTER 8

THOMAS DECIDES

Early the next morning Thomas was awoken by one of the king's valets who brought him a fine new suit of clothes.

"The king says, put on these clothes and wait for him to send a message. When he is ready to see you, go at once to the Throne Room," announced the valet. "If you wish, I am to stay and help you to dress."

"Thank you," replied Thomas, "I should be very grateful for your help. I have never worn such fine clothes before."

When he was properly dressed in his new finery he sat on the edge of his bed waiting for the king's message. He was now quite clear in his mind what he was going to reply to the king's offer.

When Thomas entered the Throne Room, the king looked at him with a very stern expression.

"Well, Thomas, what is it to be? Do you stay and learn to be a king, or will you go and marry your farm girl – and be a peasant as you were before?"

"May it please Your Majesty," said Thomas firmly, "I must go."

"It doesn't please me at all," said the king in an angry voice. "Haven't you learned that it is dangerous to displease a king? What if I were to order you to stay, and throw you into prison if you disobey?"

"I am very sorry that you are displeased and angry, Your Majesty," replied Thomas, "especially as you have been so kind to me all the time I have been in your service. If you were to put me in prison, I should bear my punishment patiently, and live for the day when you would set me free and allow me to go home."

"Very well," said the king, even more angrily than before.

"You do not value your freedom, let us see whether you value your life. Kneel down here in front of me!" As he was saying this, the king drew his sword. "If you do not carry out my command, I can cut off your head with one stroke of this sharp sword. Now, once again, will you go, or will you stay?"

"I must go – either home, by your leave, or to meet my maker in Heaven, should I be good enough to go there."

"Close your eyes," ordered the king.

Thomas did so.

The sword flashed in the morning light as the king raised it high above his head – and brought it down gently on Thomas's right shoulder, then his left.

"Open your eyes," said the king.

Thomas looked with astonishment – not only was he still alive, but the king was actually smiling. "Congratulations, Thomas," said the king in quite a different voice from his previous angry tone. "You have passed all the tests, and shown me that you really love your Gerda, and that you are determined to keep your promise to her. Now that I have dubbed you with my sword, you are no longer plain Thomas, but Sir Thomas of the Shining Kingdom – and all in this palace shall respect your new rank. And by the way…" he continued with an even broader smile and a twinkle in his eyes, "I was only pretending to be angry. I think I did it quite well, don't you?"

Thomas was too shocked and surprised to say anything except, "Thank you, Your Majesty…"

"Go back to your room, Thomas, and collect your wits," said the king. "You may set off for home in a few days, but till then, you have much to learn about your new situation. You are a good boy and you have done well. I heartily wish that you were staying. But a king, too, must keep his promises."

When Thomas had left, the king called a servant and sent him to tell the squiremaster to attend the Throne Room at once.

"My young servant Thomas, is to be a knight," the king told the squiremaster. "He must learn in days what your young squires learn in years. He is intelligent and hard-working and deserves his advancement."

"With respect, Your Majesty," answered the old squiremaster, "what you ask is quite impossible."

"Kings sometimes ask their subjects to do the impossible," replied the king, "and subjects must obey. So find young Thomas, and begin your work at once. Or perhaps you are getting too old to be squiremaster, and you would like to retire, and end your days cleaning out the stables?"

"I will try to carry out your command, Your Majesty," said the squiremaster hastily. "I have no wish to retire."

"Go, then!" ordered the king sharply.

Without further words the squiremaster bowed, and left the Throne Room in search of Thomas.

CHAPTER 9

THE LETTER

Thomas soon realised that it would be weeks rather than days before he learned all that the squiremaster had to teach him. So he decided to send another letter to Gerda, telling her the good news. When Thomas asked the Lord Chancellor to send the letter as he had done before, he spoke to Thomas like this:

"Sir Thomas, you are now too important a man to send letters in the ordinary way. I shall choose a servant to be your messenger, and he shall have a swift horse, and take your message wherever you wish it to go."

This is what Thomas wrote:

My dearest Gerda,

I am writing to tell you of my good fortune. The king has given me money and great honour, and I shall now be able to come home and keep my promise to marry you. We shall be able to have our own house and live happily together. I must tell you too, that I have found our ring. You will hardly believe how this happened, but you will have to wait till I come home to hear the story. I'm sure you must have lost our ring by accident or had it stolen, so you must not worry about it any more. Think of it, Gerda! The chancellor has chosen a special messenger to carry my letter to you! Please ask Wilhelm to give him food and a night's lodging, as he will have a long ride back to this kingdom. Now he is waiting to set out, so I must seal the letter. We shall be together very soon.

This comes with all my love, from your Thomas.

The chancellor sent for the messenger to give him his final instructions.

"Now, listen carefully," he said. "I am trusting you to deliver this message, and I have to tell you that the king himself has ordered it to be sent. Therefore, guard it with your life, and do not for any reason fail to deliver it. If you should fail, it would be better if you never showed your face in this kingdom again. I should personally make sure that the king ordered you to be locked up in the deepest dungeon for the rest of your days!"

The messenger only replied, "Yes, Your Excellency," but he thought to himself, *There's no need to threaten me. I have a good horse, enough money to stay in decent inns on the way, and careful instructions about where to go and who is to receive the letter. There's no reason why I shouldn't deliver it safely.*

Soon the messenger was riding out of the palace gates on his journey to Wilhelm's farm, to deliver Thomas's letter. At first, all went well. Each day he covered as much ground as possible without over-tiring his horse, and each night he found an inn for a bed and food, with stabling for his horse. He enjoyed several such days riding though the pleasant countryside, covering as much ground in a few days as Thomas had done in as many months.

When he reached the city of the Prince of Schwarzberg he did not need to climb to the castle, as there was a very good inn just inside the gates. As he wore the king's badge on his shoulder, the sentry let him in immediately. He was on his way again early the next morning.

About noon on that day he entered the forest. His presence was soon noticed by the two robbers, Riese and Zwerg. They sprang on the messenger from the cover of the trees. Riese dragged him from his horse and held him tightly while Zwerg tied his wrists and ankles. They took his horse and his purse, and disappeared into the depths of the forest, leaving the messenger tied and helpless on the ground.

"There are gold pieces in here," said Zwerg excitedly, as he shook the purse.

"And we'll sell the horse for a good price in the town," said Riese.

"That was a good day's work," replied Zwerg, as they made their way to the cave where they lived.

When they opened the saddle-bag to see if the messenger was carrying anything else of value, they found Thomas's letter. As neither of them could read, they just threw it on to their cooking-fire.

At sunset a woodman who was returning to his cottage in another part of the forest found the messenger cold and hungry and tired of calling for help. The woodman treated the messenger kindly. He untied his hands and feet, rubbed his limbs until the stiffness had gone, and took him home to his cottage. There he shared his evening meal, and found him a place to sleep by the fire.

The next morning the messenger told his story to the woodman, and asked him what he should do.

"I cannot return to the king without delivering the letter," he said, "or I should be thrown into prison."

"You could go into the town and inform the watch of the robbery," the woodman suggested, "but the robbers you describe have been sought many times. Their den is so well hidden that they have never been found. In any case, the men of the watch do not often venture outside the town walls."

"I could find my way on foot to the farm where the letter was to be delivered," continued the messenger, "but I do not know what the message was, and if I arrived without it, it's certain that the king would be told."

"Then there's only one thing for you to do," said the woodman. "You must stay here in the forest and help me with my work. Hide away from all travellers and strangers, until the whole thing has been forgotten. I will give you food and a bed, and hide you when it's needed, if you will learn to cut wood and make charcoal as I do."

The messenger thought that he would prefer life in the forest, even if the work was hard, to years in the king's deepest dungeon. So he thanked the woodman for his offer, and agreed to stay with him.

★ ★ ★

Thomas had now passed all the tests set him by the squiremaster. Although the messenger had not returned, the king agreed that Thomas could set out on his journey home.

On the evening before he began his journey, the king sent for Thomas, and spoke to him thus:

"Thomas, you know that all my servants wear my badge on their shoulders as you do now. But I am going to give you a special badge, which you see here."

"This badge, as you see," continued the king, "bears a picture of the sun, painted in gold. When you wear it, you become an Honorary Prince of the Shining Kingdom, and hold a higher rank than any prince or nobleman in the land, except of course, myself and the queen. You need not wear it always. Sometimes it might be more convenient to present yourself as a knight, or even as a poor farmer as you were before. The choice is yours."

The next morning Thomas mounted the fine horse that the king had given him, and turning to salute the queen and the princesses who were waving from their window, left the palace.

CHAPTER 10

TROUBLE AT THE FARM

Gerda no longer waited at the gate each day after her work. She had almost forgotten the song they used to sing together. But she still remembered Thomas and had never given up hope that one day he would return. As for the ring, she still felt very guilty about losing it. She hoped that Thomas would be so pleased to see her, when he returned, that he would soon forgive her.

Then trouble struck the farm. One morning Wilhelm had an accident. He was feeding the cattle in the barn when he fell awkwardly on the cobbled floor. He found that he could not move without great pain, and realised that his right leg was broken.

Robert and Gerda had already left the house to work in the fields. Gertrud was churning butter in the dairy, and did not hear Wilhelm's cries for help. Not until she had finished the churning, and was crossing the farmyard to return to the house did she realise that something was wrong.

Opening the barn door, she found Wilhelm lying on

the floor, by now too weak with pain and shock to utter more than a faint cry. His face was so pale and drawn that she thought he must be near to death. Although greatly upset to find her husband hurt and in so much pain, she knew what she must do.

"I cannot lift you by myself," she told him. "Robert and Gerda are in the fields. I shall take the horse and ride to the village for help."

Before she set out, Gertrud made Wilhelm as comfortable as possible. She brought a pillow and blankets from the farmhouse, and covered him to prevent him taking cold. Then as quickly as possible she saddled the horse.

"Keep your spirits up," she said to Wilhelm, kissing his cold cheek. "I shall be back with help soon." She mounted the horse and Wilhelm heard hoofbeats dying away in the distance.

A very long time seemed to pass before Wilhelm heard sounds of horses approaching. Gertrud had gone to the convent for help. When the prioress heard what had happened, she sent two of the lay brothers with a horse and a flat four-wheeled cart to take Wilhelm to the infirmary at the convent. There he would be cared for.

The brothers piled hay on their cart to make a soft bed. They tied Wilhelm's broken leg with two stout pieces of wood to prevent the broken bones from moving. Then they lifted him gently on to the cart, and set off to the convent.

Soon Wilhelm was in one of the beds in the infirmary,

where he was made as comfortable as possible. The apothecary had made up a soothing herbal drink that would help to dull the pain, and one of the nuns helped him to sip this.

The prioress drew Gertrud aside, and spoke seriously to her:

"Your husband is of an age when a broken leg is a danger to life. We will try our best to make him well again, but we cannot be sure that he will recover. If he does, it will take a long time."

Wilhelm had been a strong, healthy man all his life. Also, he was determined to be back on the farm. So the nuns were amazed at his progress. Within a few weeks he was well enough to return home, but he could take little part in the work of the farm. He could only hobble about with the help of two sticks. Gertrud thought with dismay that he looked years older since his accident, although of course she did not tell him so.

During all this time, the work of the farm had to go on. Fortunately it was not a very busy time of the year, but the work on a farm is never done. Gerda, Robert and Gertrud had been working even harder than usual.

Now Wilhelm was back home, they hoped that he would gradually be able to take his share of the work. But weeks went by, and he showed little sign of improvement.

One evening after supper, they were all sitting quietly in the big farmhouse kitchen. Wilhelm had been very quiet throughout the meal. Suddenly he spoke.

"Something must be done," he said, firmly.

No one spoke, as they could see that something very serious was afoot, so Robert, Gerda and Gertrud listened quietly to what Wilhelm had to say.

"I have come to realise that my days as a farmer are over," said Wilhelm sadly. "I can no longer do a day's work. Gertrud is wearing herself out looking after me and trying to help with the farm work at the same time. So something must be done."

Wilhelm paused. "Put another log on the fire, Gerda, and I will tell you what I have in mind."

When Gerda had made up the log fire, Wilhelm made himself as comfortable as he could in his chair, and continued:

"You all know that by the coppice in the south field there is a small cottage, that no-one has lived in since my old father died, years ago. I shall have this cottage made ready, and then Gertrud and I will live there. We shall grow a few vegetables and herbs, and keep a few chickens and geese; and there we will end our days in peace."

Gerda felt a tear trickling down her cheek at the thought of Wilhelm and Gertrud leaving the farmhouse.

"Do not cry, Gerda," said Wilhelm kindly, "we shall not be far away, and we are both good for many years yet."

Now Wilhelm turned to Robert. "You, my son, will be in charge of the farm. Gerda will keep house for you, and we will hire a man from the village, who is willing to work on the farm each day and return home at night.

I have taught you all I know about the work of the farm, and I'm sure you will make a success of it."

"But Wilhelm," said Gerda, "what will happen when Thomas comes home?"

Wilhelm looked at her sadly. "I do not know how to tell you this, but after such a long time I very much fear that he will never return."

Gerda was very shocked by this remark. "Do you know something? Have you had news?" she cried. "Is there bad news that I should know?"

"Calm yourself," replied Wilhelm gently. "We have had no news. We know no more than you do. But after so many years and months you should prepare yourself for the worst. Perhaps you should try to forget about him."

"I could never forget him," Gerda burst out, her tears flowing more freely now.

Now Robert spoke for the first time. He was a quiet, thoughtful young man, and was very fond of Gerda. He tried very hard to comfort her.

"Dear Gerda," he said quietly, "do not upset yourself. If Thomas returns, we shall welcome him like a long-lost brother. There will always be a place for him on the farm. What you will do if you are married, I cannot tell. It will depend on his wishes, and on his situation. In the meantime, you and I have always been like brother and sister, and that we shall always be."

At this, Gerda stopped crying and became calmer.

So the family continued to discuss the details of

Wilhelm's plan, and before bedtime that night had agreed that on the very next day, Robert would ride into the town, and find a thatcher who would come and make the roof of the cottage weather-proof, and a builder who would do various repairs to make it fit to live in once more.

★ ★ ★

Just before Wilhelm and Gertrud moved into their cottage, now cosy and comfortable, they had a visit from the parish priest. Father Paulus was an old friend, and had known Robert and Gerda since they were very young children. He had visited Wilhelm in the convent infirmary when he was seriously ill, and was pleased to see him looking so much better. But when he heard what they planned to do, his face grew very serious.

"Listen, my old friend," said Father Paulus quietly. "It is good that you and your wife should retire from the hard work of the farm, and live quietly in your cottage. But you must not allow Robert and Gerda to live together in the farmhouse unless they are married. The Church would regard that as a great sin."

"But why?" asked Wilhelm. "They have always been like brother and sister, and that is how they will always be."

"That may be so," answered the priest. "But Gerda is adopted. She is really no relation to Robert. So it would be just the same as if they were complete strangers."

Wilhelm was taken aback by what Father Paulus had to say. He imagined all his plans for the future in ruins. He turned to the priest. "Then what can we do?" he asked.

"Two things are possible," he replied gravely. "Either they must get married, even though it might be a marriage in name only. Or, a reliable lady of mature age must be found, who would live in the farmhouse with them."

When the priest had left, Wilhelm sent for Gerda and explained what Father Paulus had said. He also made it clear to her that marriage was the only way.

"We are already paying a man to work on the farm," he said. "There is no way that I could also pay a woman to live in the house. There is still no word from Thomas, nor any sign of his returning. So, for my sake and Gertrud's, will you consider marrying Robert?"

Wilhelm looked so worried, his face white and drawn. Gerda was afraid that the worry would make him ill again. So she promised that she would go away and think seriously about it, and give her answer the next day.

Next morning she sought out Wilhelm and not without a few tears, spoke to him thus: "Dear Wilhelm, you and Gertrud have loved me and surrounded me with kindness all my life, and I would hate to do anything to make you unhappy. I still love my Thomas dearly, but I am beginning to believe that you are right, and that he will never return. So I am asking you if you are able to hire someone to live in the house with us for just a few weeks. If Thomas has not returned by Easter Day, I will marry Robert."

CHAPTER 11

A SHOCK FOR THE PECULIAR PRINCE

Thomas had been journeying on, making good progress towards home. When he stayed the night at an inn, he always asked for news of the messenger.

"Has a horseman passed this way, wearing the badge of the King of the Shining Kingdom?" he would ask.

Many times he had the reply, "Yes, he travelled to the south some weeks ago, but he has not returned."

He must be staying a while at the farm, thought Thomas. *I expect they will not let him leave until he has told them all he knows about me, and about the kingdom.* All the same, he did wonder why the messenger was staying so long, as the king and the Lord Chancellor would be awaiting his early return.

It was late in the afternoon, when Thomas was thinking about finding lodgings for the night, that he saw a familiar castle on a hill in the distance. Thomas recognised it as the castle of the Prince of Schwarzberg, the one whom he had called the 'Peculiar Prince'. He remembered that this was the man who spied on his subjects and who had thrown him into the dungeons. He smiled to himself as he thought what he would do. He fixed on his shoulder the badge that the king had given him, which showed him to be prince of the Shining Kingdom, and higher in rank than any other prince.

I shall ride up to the castle, he thought to himself, *and demand a special banquet to be prepared. I shall sleep in the best bed in the castle, even if it means turning that sly prince out of his own chamber.* But as it happened, things turned out rather differently, and the Peculiar Prince was made even more uncomfortable than Thomas had planned.

The soldier at the city gate made no attempt to stop Thomas entering. He did not even shout "Halt!" but opened the gate wide and bowed his head as Thomas passed inside. Once inside the city, he dismounted, and as his horse had travelled many miles that day, led him slowly up the steep, cobbled street.

I wonder whether the beggar is still here, thought Thomas. *If he is, I shall reward him with a piece of gold, as he warned me about the Prince when I was a poor traveller.*

But as he approached the place where the beggar had been sitting, he stopped and looked very hard. Yes, there was a beggar sitting in the same place as before, but it was not the same one. Thomas looked at him even more carefully, and this time he was sure: it was the prince in disguise.

I'll teach him a lesson, thought Thomas. Then he drew his sword, and, approaching the beggar, held the point of the sword to his chest, and called out in a loud voice, "Call out the guard! Call out the guard!"

Three soldiers appeared almost immediately.

"Arrest this man!" ordered Thomas, "and take him to the castle dungeons."

"Excuse me, Your Highness," said the sergeant of the guard, "but begging is allowed in this city."

"That may be so, sergeant," said Thomas sternly, "but only for those who are so poor that they need to beg. This man is cheating the townspeople: he has more money than you have."

By now a small crowd had gathered, curious to see what was happening.

"Take off his shirt!" ordered Thomas. The sergeant pulled it off, and showed that underneath the shirt, the so-called beggar was wearing a richly embroidered silk undergarment.

There were angry sounds from the crowd, and cries of "Off to prison with him!"

By now the Peculiar Prince had recovered from his surprise.

"Stop all this at once, sergeant," he cried. "I am the Prince of Schwarzberg!"

At this there were roars of laughter from the crowd.

"Yes, of course you are," replied the sergeant, "and I am the Angel Gabriel, and you and I are going to take a short walk up to the castle." Still protesting, the prince was marched off by the soldiers. If anyone in the crowd had recognised the prince, no one was saying.

Thomas followed them up the hill to the castle, where he arranged that the prince should be put into the same cell where he himself had spent the night on his last visit to the castle. Then he presented himself at the main door, where the steward showed him into the Great Hall. Here he was politely greeted by the princess.

"I am very sorry that my husband is not here to welcome you," she said, "but he often has to go on important journeys and has to be away for some days at a time."

It was clear that his wife did not know of the prince's spying activities, and Thomas thought it best not to tell her.

"I hope you are able to stay till he returns," continued the princess, "and I will order the very best guest room to be made ready for you. Then perhaps you will do me the honour of being my guest for supper."

So Thomas, who had been a poor farm boy, dined with the princess, and was not ill at ease, as he had been taught before he left the Shining Kingdom how a person of his rank should behave.

A wonderful banquet had been prepared, and before he retired to the comfort of the large four-poster bed in the guest room, Thomas asked whether he could congratulate the cook on the quality of the meal he had enjoyed.

"Certainly," said the princess, "I will send for him at once and perhaps you will then excuse me if I retire to my bed. I hope you sleep well, and I hope to see you in the morning."

"I cannot promise that," replied Thomas. "I have a long day's ride before me tomorrow, and I must set out at dawn. So if I do not see you, I thank you for your hospitality. Please give my regards to your husband when he returns. Perhaps he will be back tomorrow, and so, goodnight."

Soon after the princess had left, the cook came into the room. Of course, he did not recognise Thomas as the boy who had worked in his kitchen and had been thrown into prison by the prince.

The cook bowed. "Your Highness sent for me?"

"Look at my face!" ordered Thomas. The cook did so, and as he recognised who it was, gave a gasp of surprise.

"Yes, it is really I," said Thomas. "I have had great good fortune, and I am now really what I appear to be – the greatest prince in the land."

The cook was too surprised to reply.

"When I was here before," continued Thomas, "you were kind to me. You gave me work when I badly needed it. You let me out of prison as soon as you were able. So I am going to give you ten gold pieces as a reward. There is a man in the same cell in which I was imprisoned. You are to let him out early tomorrow morning. As you do so you are to say these words to him: 'One night only, that is fair'. Will you do this?"

"Yes, Your Highness, I will do it," said the cook. "But

what if my prince is angry because I have let a prisoner go free?"

"I can tell you," replied Thomas, "that your prince will be only too pleased that you have let this man free."

When Thomas had given the cook the gold pieces he had promised, he dismissed him and went to bed.

He arose before dawn, collected his horse from the stables, and was on his way before anyone in the castle was awake.

CHAPTER 12

THE ROBBERS

As Thomas approached the forest, he was feeling quite pleased with himself. Perhaps he was a little too pleased with himself. He was still smiling as he pictured the Peculiar Prince being released from prison by the cook. When the ring on his chest began to tremble, he took little heed. He recognised it as a warning, but thought to himself, *I passed through the forest before, when I was on foot and unarmed; now I am a knight on horseback. Besides, the only way to avoid the forest is to take the mountain track, making my journey two whole days longer.* He drew his sword and urged his horse onward. He would bitterly regret ignoring the ring's warning.

The two robbers, Zwerg and Riese, had been on the look-out for rich travellers. When they saw Thomas approaching, they knew at once that here was someone with money and rich clothing. When they were dealing with someone on foot, or someone leading his horse as the messenger had done, they jumped out on their victim from behind the trees. But when someone was riding a horse, as Thomas was, they had another plan.

First they went ahead to a place on the forest track where the traveller would soon arrive. Zwerg climbed a tall tree that had a branch directly over the path. Riese hid behind the tree. When Zwerg heard the sounds of the horse's hoofs approaching, he hung from the branch by his arms, and began to swing to and fro.

Thomas walked his horse carefully along the rough forest track. He kept looking left and right for any sign of danger, but did not look upwards. He did not imagine that an attack could come down from above. He still felt a strange tingling sensation on his chest, but he thought nothing of it.

Crash!

Just as Thomas passed underneath him, Zwerg dropped from the branch, pulling him from his horse on to the ground. His sword flew out of his hand, and before he could recover from the fall, Riese jumped out and pinned him to the ground. When they had stripped him of his purse and most of his clothing, they left him tied to the tree, wrapped in a rough old cloak that Riese had been wearing. Then, leading his horse and carrying his belongings, they set off to return to their cave. They had intended to leave Thomas in the forest, just as they had treated the messenger.

They had not gone very far before they were curious to know what Thomas's saddlebag contained. Among his belongings they were amazed to find the badge of the Prince of the Shining Kingdom, which Zwerg recognised.

"Do you realise who this is?" he asked his companion.

"We have captured someone really important. We must keep him safely in the cave until we can send a message to the king. We could be paid more gold than we can imagine for his release. We could retire from being robbers and live in comfort for the rest of our lives."

So the two robbers returned to where Thomas was tied. They unfastened his legs, blindfolded him, and led him through the forest to their cave.

When they reached the cave, they uncovered his eyes. Thomas was amazed to look around him and see that the cave was very large, and was furnished with a table and chairs. By the light of several candles, which stood on the table in empty wine bottles, he could see all around. He noticed, at the far end of the cave, an opening, which seemed to lead to a smaller cave. He looked towards the entrance to see if there was any possibility of escape, but only saw Riese fixing a heavy wooden grille over the mouth of the cave, and fastening it with chains and locks to staples driven into the stone.

"You will not be tied while you are in the cave," said Riese to Thomas. "You can see that it is useless to try to escape."

"You can think yourself very lucky, sir knight, or my lord, whoever you may be," added Zwerg. "If you had been an ordinary person, we should have left you in the forest. There you would have stayed until someone came along who was stupid enough to set you free."

"But I might have died," exclaimed Thomas. "I might have starved to death or been eaten by wolves."

"Bad luck!" said Zwerg. "When we have robbed someone, they are no more use to us."

"So you are murderers as well as robbers!" said Thomas angrily.

"Oh no, we never actually kill anyone," replied Zwerg. "But if they die by accident, well, we can't help that, can we?"

Thomas was silent for a while. "In that case, why have you brought me here?"

"Because," answered Riese, "we can see that you are a person of some importance. You wear the king's badge. So we are going to keep you here until the king pays us to set you free. You will be given food and a place to sleep, and we shall treat you well, but of course we cannot let you go until we have sent a message to the king, and he has paid the ransom that we ask."

That was the beginning of a long, weary time for Thomas. Every day the robbers set out for the forest to watch out for travellers. Riese never forgot to block the mouth of the cave with the wooden grille, and lock it in place. Some days they returned in the evening laughing and shouting, with food and bottles of wine. But many nights they returned sadly with sour faces, when no travellers had passed through the forest.

Sometimes the robbers boasted about all the rich

people they had robbed, and from listening to what they said, Thomas discovered that they had robbed the king's messenger and left him in the forest. This news made Thomas very worried, as he realised that his letter could never have been delivered to Gerda.

But another piece of news was more cheering. One day Zwerg announced that he had found a peasant who would take a message to the king, in return for five gold pieces. Luckily the robbers had not spent all the gold pieces in Thomas's purse, so they were able to send the peasant on his way. To prove to the king that Thomas really was a prisoner, they made the man take with him Thomas's badge, the badge of the Prince of the Shining Kingdom.

The robbers also gave the peasant a donkey on which to ride to the king's palace. Thomas heard them talking outside the cave.

"Here are your five pieces of gold," Zwerg was saying. "The king will give you at least five more when you give him the message. Don't forget, now: he must send five thousand gold pieces to us before we will set this prisoner free. And get there as quickly as you can. The autumn is coming on, and we need an answer before the winter."

"And don't try to run off with the money," added Riese, "because we shall find you wherever you hide, and I shall cut you into bite-sized pieces and feed you to the dogs."

The robbers did not really have any dogs, but what Riese said was quite enough to frighten the simple countryman, who mounted the donkey and set off down the track which led to the forest.

Riese and Zwerg did not realise what a great distance it was to the Shining Kingdom. When two or three weeks had gone by, they expected a message from the king, with five thousand gold pieces. Every day one of them rode on Thomas's horse through the forest and some way along the track to the north, to see if anyone was approaching.

As they thought that very soon they would be rich, they did not go out into the forest and lie in wait for travellers. The weeks went by, the trees lost their leaves and the first snows of winter fell. Few travellers now ventured on journeys. For these reasons the robbers spent more and more time in the cave, playing dice and drinking wine. From time to time, when the weather allowed, one of them would ride Thomas's horse into the town, to sell some stolen item, and bring back food and more bottles of wine. Sometimes they would go out to collect firewood.

Even when they were in the cave, they spoke very little to Thomas, who suffered from loneliness and boredom. He began to wonder whether he would ever escape, and whether he would ever see his Gerda again.

CHAPTER 13

ZWERG FINDS THE SNAKE RING

So the winter passed. Some days the robbers took Thomas out into the forest to help them to collect firewood, but always with a chain around his waist, the other end securely by Riese. Sometimes, if there was a break in the weather, they would go out looking for travellers. But even when the snow melted, and signs of spring began to appear in the forest, no travellers passed by. Food was short, and all that remained in the cave was a small supply of salted meat, and a few dry biscuits full of maggots. Anything that was worth selling was already sold.

One day Thomas overheard the robbers whispering to each other in the small cave where they slept. They did not realise this, but their voices were reflected by the stone walls, and could be heard clearly by Thomas in the larger chamber.

"Let's kill him," Riese was saying. "We are not going

to get any money from the king. There's barely enough food for two, and only starvation diet for three!"

"I think we should wait a bit longer," replied Zwerg. "We should feel foolish if the ransom money arrived tomorrow, or the next day."

"The peasant may have deceived us," said Riese, "so maybe the king doesn't know anything about it. So no-one will be any wiser if there's just one more grave in the forest."

"Hardly anyone travels in the winter," answered Zwerg. "Even now we could have more snow to block the tracks. I suggest that we wait until Easter, and if the money hasn't come by then, I agree, we should kill him."

Thomas had to pretend that he had not overheard what the robbers were saying. He realised that he was in greater danger than at any time since he was brought to the cave. Yet he could think of no way to escape.

Later that same day, something happened that made Thomas very unhappy. But as he discovered later, it removed the immediate danger. All the time he had lived with the robbers in the cave, Thomas had managed to keep the snake-ring hidden. The robbers had taken all his clothes and belongings, except a cross made of polished wood, which hung round his neck on a leather thong. The robbers had not thought this worth selling. Besides, in those days, even robbers had enough respect for religion to leave such an object alone. They believed that bad luck would befall them, if they stole a holy object.

Before he left the Shining Kingdom, Thomas had hidden the snake-ring by melting a small piece of beeswax, and using this to fasten the ring to the back of the cross. In the cave he had taken care to keep the cross under the old shirt that the robbers had given him to wear. When he stripped off his shirt to wash, he had made sure that the side of the cross that held the ring was turned towards his chest.

Thomas was thinking so hard about what he had just heard, and trying desperately to think of a way of escape, that he forgot to think of the ring.

"What's this, then?" Riese cried out in a mocking voice.

Thomas looked down and realised that the ring was in full view. Riese reached out and snatched the ring. "Thought you were clever, did you? Kept your best jewel till the last, eh?"

"Come and look at this!" he called to Zwerg. "Here's something that's worth a few loaves of bread and bottles of wine! Something that will keep us alive till the king's ransom arrives!"

"Please don't take it," begged Thomas. "It's a keepsake from my sweetheart, and it's not worth very much."

"Don't lie," said Zwerg, who took the ring from Riese and turned it this way and that in his fingers, making the jewels glint in the light. "I've stolen lots of precious things in my time, and I know gold when I see it."

"Look for yourself," said Thomas despairingly. "You

73

will see my name and my sweetheart's written on it. Look on the snakes' tails!"

"I can see some marks," said Riese.

"Don't believe him," replied Zwerg. "He's only trying to trick us because he knows we can't read. Let's sell the ring in the town – I can't wait to get some good food and wine inside me."

It was too late to set out on a journey to the town that day. Next morning, when Riese pulled back the furs that covered the grille at the mouth of the cave, he saw that it had snowed during the night. In spite of this, the robbers decided to start out on their journey. As they had sold Thomas's horse some time ago, they would have to walk to the town. They put on their warmest clothing, took the little food that was left, and set off into the forest without a word to Thomas.

CHAPTER 14

A WEDDING IS PREPARED

Spring was late coming that year. It was already Lent –
the time just before Easter – but a sprinkling of snow still
covered the land.

The farm had prospered. The hired man had been a
hard worker, and Dame Margaret, the kind lady from the
village who had come to live with Robert and Gerda in
the farmhouse, had grown quite fond of the two young
people and had demanded no payment. She said she
would be sorry to leave when they were married.

Every evening when the farm work was over, and
supper had been eaten and cleared away, Robert would
sit at the table with a book which Father Paulus had lent
him. Dame Margaret would be doing the household
mending, and Gerda would sit sewing her wedding dress.
As she did so, she could not help shedding a few tears
from time to time. These days she was much quieter and
more serious, and it was a long time since she had sung
the little song that she and Thomas used to sing together.

Wilhelm and Gertrud were still living quietly and

contentedly in their little cottage by the coppice. One day, soon after the beginning of Lent, Father Paulus rode up to the farm on his pony. First, he sought out Robert, who was cutting wood in the barn.

When he had greeted him warmly, he asked after the health of Wilhelm and Gertrud. Then he came to the main purpose of his visit.

"It is time we fixed a date for your wedding," he said. "You know that weddings cannot take place in Lent, but I am going to suggest to your parents that we arrange it for the first day after Easter. Are you in agreement with that?"

Robert looked very seriously at the priest. "To tell you the truth, Father, I am beginning to have doubts about this marriage. You know that my feelings for Gerda are those of a brother, not a lover. Besides, there is something else."

The priest looked puzzled. "What could that possibly be?" he asked.

"You have lent me several books to read of late," replied Robert, "books about religion and the Church and I have begun to think seriously about becoming a priest myself. I realise that I should have to go away to a seminary and study very hard. But, of course, if I were married I could never do this."

"If you would let me advise you," said Father Paulus, "even though it is a great service to God to become a priest, I think your duty lies here, on this farm. Your parents are depending on you, now they cannot work on the farm. And I think that for you, a marriage of friendship will be better than no marriage at all. The life of a priest can be very lonely, as I know very well."

The two men sat quietly together for a while without speaking, then Robert said quietly, "I think you are right, Father. The first day after Easter, then." And he turned away sadly, and continued his work without another word.

Father Paulus next sought out Gerda, who was helping Dame Margaret to make soup in the kitchen.

"I have just spoken to Robert," began the priest, "and he has agreed to the first day after Easter as your wedding day. Do you agree to that too?"

"You know my feelings," answered Gerda sadly, "and you know that I have promised Wilhelm and Gertrud that I will do this for their sake. So I agree. But they know, and you must know too, that if Thomas returns before then, I am free of my promise, and he is the man that I will marry."

"I am very sorry for you, my child," said the priest. "You must have a very great love for him to have waited all this time. It saddens me to tell you, that I do not think there is any hope of his returning. Either he cannot return or does not wish to. So I advise you to make the most of what your life offers. As I told Robert, a marriage of friendship is better than no marriage at all."

The priest then rode down to the cottage, where he found Wilhelm and Gertrud. Not wishing to upset them, he did not tell them about the doubts in the minds of

Robert and Gerda, but said that they had both agreed to the date he had suggested.

The old people were almost overcome with joy. "At last!" said Wilhelm. "What we've always wished for is coming true."

"We must have a great supper in the barn," said Gertrud, "and invite all our friends and neighbours to be happy with us."

Father Paulus was very thoughtful as he rode home, and when he said his Mass that night, he was careful to say a special prayer for the happiness of the young people at the farm.

CHAPTER 15

THE ROBBERS ARE CAUGHT

It was late in the day when the two robbers reached the town. They were weary with trudging through the snow, and they were also very hungry. As they had no money to buy food or pay for a night's lodging, they decided to sell the snake-ring as quickly as possible. There was an inn next to the church, and Zwerg asked the innkeeper for directions.

"There are two goldsmiths' shops in the town," was the reply. "A large one by the north gate, that's about half a mile up the road, and a small one, just behind the church, just five minutes' walk from here."

Immediately after Riese heard this, he shouted, "The big one! The big one for a better price!"

Usually, if there was a difference of opinion between the two of them, it was Riese who won the argument. This time it was strangely different.

"No! No!" cried Zwerg, "I'm dog tired, I'm hungry. I

can't walk another half a mile. Even this ring on my finger feels as if it weighs a ton. So we must go to the small one."

Riese was too amazed by his companion's unusual behaviour to reply. "Come along then," said Zwerg, who seemed to have regained his strength. A few minutes later they arrived at the goldsmith's shop.

"Now we must be on our best behaviour," said Zwerg. "Speak gently to the man, let him think we are honest travellers who have run out of money. We shall get more for it that way."

Riese only grunted. It was not his way of going about things, but he had just enough sense to realise that his companion was right. "Very well," he agreed at length. "I'll leave you to do the talking."

"Good evening, gentlemen," said the goldsmith. "What can I do for you?"

"We wondered whether you would be interested in buying this ring," said Zwerg. "We have a long way to travel, and have run out of money."

When the goldsmith took the ring in his hand to examine it, he almost dropped it in surprise. For he was the very same goldsmith who had engraved the names of Thomas and Gerda, and of course, he recognised the ring immediately.

"This is a very remarkable ring," he said to the robbers. "May I ask you how it came into your hands?"

Riese was just about to say "Mind your own business," when Zwerg dug him in the ribs to remind him to keep quiet.

"Of course," said Zwerg pleasantly. "It belonged to a young man who owed us money, and we took the ring to settle his debt. He was unwilling to part with it, but he had no other possessions, and my friend here gets very impatient with people who owe us money."

The goldsmith looked at the size and strength of Riese, and thought to himself, *Perhaps young Thomas might have given up his ring to these men. But they may be robbers who have stolen the ring, and if so I mean to see them punished.*

So he said to the robbers, "You are right in thinking that ring is worth a great deal of money, and I am willing to pay you the proper price for it. But I do not keep such a large sum of money here in my workshop. So I suggest that you come back as soon as I open my workshop tomorrow morning. I will bring a large bag of gold pieces, and we can agree on the price."

The robbers looked at one another as though they were uncertain what to do. Then the goldsmith went behind his counter and brought out five gold pieces. He handed Zwerg the ring, and said, "Take back the ring for the present and take this money on account. It is enough to buy you a very good meal and a comfortable night in the best room at the inn. Then in the morning we will do business together."

Zwerg took the ring. Both the robbers looked greedily at the gold, and they thought about good food and wine, and a comfortable bed. "We agree," said Riese, picking up the gold.

"Till the morning, then," added Zwerg, as they left the goldsmith's workshop.

"That was a good idea," said Riese, as they set off towards the inn.

"Perhaps it was," replied Zwerg, "but what if the goldsmith suspects us? What if we arrive there in the morning and he has guards hiding in the back room?"

"What if he has?" asked Riese. "I can deal with a few guards. It would take twenty men to capture me!"

"I have a better idea," said Zwerg. "This is what we do. At the inn tonight, we find out where the goldsmith lives. Then, early tomorrow morning, before it is light, we creep out of the inn and steal two horses from the stables. Then we go to the goldsmith's house. We break in and take his gold, and ride off before anyone else is awake."

"That's brilliant!" said Riese admiringly. "I wish I had brains like you."

"And I wish that I was strong like you," said Zwerg. "But together we make a good pair."

The goldsmith had made sure that he had given the robbers enough money to eat and drink well. In fact, they drank a little too well, so that it was not long before they were both in a deep sleep. Riese was snoring loudly.

The goldsmith did not go home when he locked up his workshop. He went to the house of the chief magistrate of the town. He explained about the visit from the robbers, and why he thought that the ring was stolen.

"Where are they now?" asked the magistrate.

"I gave them money for food and a night's lodging at the inn," replied the goldsmith, "and I should be very surprised if they are not there at this moment."

"I am very interested in these two men," said the magistrate. "We have had reports for some time now of two robbers, one big and strong, and the other small and wiry, who have been preying on travellers as they passed through the forest. We have never been able to discover where they hide, deep in the forest. If these are the same men, they must be captured at once. There is a valuable reward for information leading to their arrest."

The magistrate then sent for the captain of the guard, and explained to him that the robbers were at the inn, and must be captured. "If they still have the ring, we could arrest them for possessing stolen property. Then we could find other witnesses who would recognise them."

"If the big robber is so strong," said the captain, "it would be best to creep into the inn at midnight and take them while they are asleep."

The goldsmith went home to his supper and a peaceful sleep, but for the robbers it was quite different. The captain and six guards moved quietly up the stairs of the inn. The captain held a shaded lantern, and by its light two guards stood by Riese's head, and two by his feet, while the other two stood by Zwerg. The captain gave the order to begin, and five minutes later it was all over. Before they were even properly awake, the robbers were securely tied and transported to the town lock-up.

The next morning, their appointment was not kept with the goldsmith, but before the magistrates in court.

News spread quickly round the town that two notorious robbers had been caught, and were to be tried at noon. By the time the magistrates took their places on the bench, and the robbers were brought from the prison, the courthouse was full of people.

"You are accused of having in your possession stolen property, namely a ring. Are you guilty or not guilty?"

"Not guilty!" said the robbers together.

"Who accuses these men of robbery?" asked the chief magistrate.

The goldsmith stepped forward. "I do, your honour. They came into my workshop offering to sell me a ring. I know that it belonged to a young man, who had his name and the name of his sweetheart, engraved on it. He would never have sold it or given it to these men."

"What were the names?" asked the magistrate.

"Thomas and Gerda," replied the goldsmith.

"Does anyone here know these persons?"

A man on the front row of the crowd raised his hand. "Your honour," he said, "I knew Thomas when he used to work at Riverside Farm. But he went on a journey many months ago, and has never returned."

The magistrate then turned to the robbers. "How do you say that you obtained the ring?"

Zwerg answered: "It did belong to a man called Thomas, but he owed us money, and gave us the ring in payment."

The magistrate then spoke to all the people present. "Can anyone here prove that these men stole the ring, and that their story is untrue?"

No one spoke.

The chief magistrate spoke quietly to the two other magistrates who sat on either side of him. "I believe they are guilty, but there is no proof. I am very sorry, but I am afraid that we shall have to let them go free."

Just at that moment, there was a commotion at the back of the courtroom as two men entered in great haste. The younger of the two men appeared to be a merchant, and the man who followed him, his servant. They walked quickly up to the bench, and the young man asked for permission to speak. When this was granted, he pointed at the two robbers and said in a loud, clear voice:

"I know these men. Their names are Riese and Zwerg, and I can swear that they are robbers, because some months ago my servant and I were captured by them in the forest. They took our money, our packhorses and our clothes, and left us tied to a tree. We were soon weak from lack of food and exposure, and would have died. But a soldier travelling home on leave found us and set us free. He bought us food and brought us safely home. My servant here can witness that what I have told you, is true."

"It is true, sir," said the servant.

"We've never seen them before!" shouted Zwerg.

"Silence!" said the magistrate. "This changes everything." He turned to Zwerg and Riese. "Is there anyone who would speak in your defence?"

There was silence. "Then I find you guilty of robbery and attempted murder," continued the magistrate. "You are to go back to prison while it is decided whether you are to be hanged or stay in prison for life. The ring shall be kept safely by the goldsmith until the true owner is found. Take them back to prison."

The guards obeyed.

CHAPTER 16

FREEDOM FOR THOMAS

Thomas was cold and hungry. The robbers had left no food in the cave, and the fire was almost out. He did not expect them to return the same day, but when they had not done so by noon on the following day, he began to suspect that something was wrong.

"I must get out of this cave," he said to himself. "But how? I've already thought of ways of escape for weeks and months, but nothing seems possible."

He found a few sticks in a corner of the cave, blew on the embers and coaxed the fire into a flame. The smoke curled upwards to the ceiling, where it found its way out through small cracks in the rock – no way out there for a man.

Through the bars of the stout wooden gate that blocked the mouth of the cave he could see the footpath leading into the forest. He grasped the bars in his hands. They were too strong to break, and too close together to squeeze through. Full of sorrow and disappointment, Thomas turned back to the fire, now blazing brightly. As he did so, an idea struck him like a flash of lightning – the fire! He could use the fire to escape!

Gathering the last few sticks of kindling wood he quickly placed them against the lower bars of the gate. He brought a burning twig from the fire, pushed it under the sticks, and soon had a useful blaze. The smoke was drawn through the bars and rose into the outside air. The bars of the gate were old and dry, and soon began to burn.

But now the fire began to die down, and Thomas looked desperately round the cave for more fuel. There was none. His eyes alighted on the small wooden chair that Zwerg usually sat on. He picked it up and dashed it against the stone wall of the cave. Fortunately, at the third or fourth blow, it splintered into pieces. Feeding the flames with the remains of the chair, he was delighted to see the fire begin to burn brightly again. Soon the bars of the gate were well alight. Thomas took the seat of the chair in both hands, and rammed the edge of it against the burning bars. They gave way, leaving a gap wide enough for a man to crawl through.

It was a tense moment, because Thomas had to wait until the fire had died down enough for him to get out without burning himself. He listened intently for any sound, which might tell him that the robbers were returning. But all was quiet, and as soon as it was safe to do so, he took one of the furs from the robbers' bed, crept through the gap in the gate, wrapped the fur around him to keep warm, and set off through the forest trees.

As it had not snowed again since the robbers had left,

their footprints could be clearly seen. At first, Thomas followed them, but soon realised that he could be in danger. If the robbers returned, they would follow the same track. So he left the path, and made his way through the trees, trying to walk on rough ground and tufts of grass, so that his own footprints showed as little as possible.

Soon Thomas was very tired. It was hard work trudging over the rough ground. It was getting colder. He had been allowed very little exercise during the time that he had been a prisoner, and for the last few days had eaten very little. Soon he was so exhausted that he lost all sense of direction, and it was not long before he realised that he was lost in the forest. When he came to a place where there was no snow, but a thick bed of dry leaves, he wanted desperately to lie down, wrap himself in his fur cloak, and go to sleep.

He sat down on the leaves, with his back to a tree, and struggled to keep awake. He remembered hearing that travellers who fall asleep in the snow never awaken.

The dream was so clear and bright. Evening sunlight fell across the hayfield and sparkled on the river beyond. Gerda was standing by the gate, beckoning to him. But the more he hurried towards her, the farther away she seemed to be, until…

Thomas awoke with a start. He could hear men shouting, and the jingle of horses' harnesses through the trees.

"It's the robbers come back," he said to himself, and

in his half-wakeful state he imagined that Riese and Zwerg must have bought horses in the town, and were riding back to the cave.

He hid behind the trees and watched, and as his senses returned he realised that there were several men in uniform leading their horses along the forest path. The procession was led by a very dignified, elderly man riding a magnificent horse.

"Help me!" cried Thomas in despair, starting to run forward towards the men. But cold and weakness and hunger overcame him, and he stumbled over a fallen branch, and fell unconscious to the ground.

CHAPTER 17

GOOD NEWS AND BAD

When Thomas came to, he was warmly wrapped in blankets in the most comfortable bed the innkeeper could provide. As he struggled to sit up, trying to piece together what had happened, a maid came into the room with a bowl of hot soup.

"The gentleman downstairs says will your honour please drink this," said the maid, making a polite curtsey. "Then, after that there's someone waiting to see you." She curtseyed again and left the room quietly.

Thomas ate his soup thoughtfully. "Who is the gentleman downstairs?" he asked himself. Perhaps it was the dignified man whom he now remembered seeing in the forest with the soldiers. And who could be waiting to see him? His heart missed a beat as he thought it might be Gerda.

A few minutes later the door of the bedroom opened again, and the innkeeper announced, in an important voice, "The king's chancellor to see you!"

Thomas was amazed. He suddenly realised that the

dignified man with the soldiers was indeed the Lord Chancellor, who had been so kind to him when he was a servant at the palace.

Seeing Thomas' surprise, the chancellor sat quietly by the bedside, took Thomas' hand in a fatherly way, and began to explain. "I should really call you 'Your Highness', but I still think of you as young Thomas, the boy I knew in the Shining Kingdom. You must know, too, that the king thinks of you as a son rather than a servant. So as soon as a message arrived, he started to make plans for your rescue."

"I was imprisoned in a robbers' cave for many long weeks," said Thomas. "I knew the king would help me if he knew, but as the time passed by I lost heart, and believed that the king had never received the message."

"The king suspected that all was not well, as the first messenger failed to return. So as soon as the worst of the winter was over, and it was possible to travel, he sent me to find you. He realised that it was useless just to send ransom money, as the villains might have taken the money and then refused to set you free. So the king sent an escort of soldiers to make sure that you were safe, and that the robbers were punished."

"They will never be caught now," answered Thomas. "They took my precious ring to sell, and left me locked in the cave without food. They will be many miles away by now." Weariness overcame him again, and he lay back on his pillows.

"We have talked too long," said the chancellor. "You

must rest now. I will come and visit you again in the morning. But you can sleep easily, because I heard some good news in the town. The robbers have been captured. They are even now in the town prison, while the magistrates decide on their punishment." He rose, and was just leaving the room when Thomas called after him.

"Did you hear any news about Gerda?"

The chancellor pretended not to hear, and closed the door. He had heard news in the town. That the beautiful Gerda, from Riverside Farm, was to marry the farmer's son, Robert, on the day following Easter Day. The chancellor did not think that Thomas had regained enough strength to hear this.

★ ★ ★

That night, Zwerg escaped from prison. It was Riese who made it possible, by using his great strength to bend one of the bars in the window. But it was only the small, slim Zwerg who could wriggle through the space.

"Don't worry," he whispered, once he was outside in the street. "I'll find a way of getting you out."

But to himself he said, "Why should I bother? He was useful while we were in the forest, but I'm better off by myself now. I shall find the goldsmith's house, steal his gold, get myself a horse and go as far away from here as I can."

★ ★ ★

Robert had been in the nearby village on farm business. While there, he had heard the news about the capture of the robbers. He had also heard that they had been keeping a young man prisoner. He was now free, but very weak and ill, and was being looked after at an inn in the town. But no one knew the young man's name, or where he came from.

On hearing this news, Gerda became both excited and fearful.

"Could it be Thomas?" she hastened to ask, "and was anything else known about him?"

"Some said he was a prince," replied Robert, "and that the king had sent an army to set him free. But others do not believe this."

"I must know!" cried Gerda. "I must go to the town now, at once!"

"It is cold and dark," answered Robert. "You cannot travel tonight. Tomorrow I will come with you. For if this man is Thomas, it changes everything for me, too."

★ ★ ★

Zwerg tethered his stolen horse among some bushes and crept quietly up to the goldsmith's house. But before he could work out how to effect an entry, he heard someone call out in a loud, deep voice: "Halt! Who goes there?"

Peering through the bushes, he saw a soldier with drawn sword advancing towards him. He ran for his life, sprang into the horse's saddle and galloped away, out of the town, into the forest. He did not stop until he reached the cave, where he was amazed to find the door broken down and the prisoner gone.

CHAPTER 18

GERDA AND ROBERT

Next morning, Thomas had eaten a hearty breakfast and was sitting up in bed, when the chancellor was announced.

He shook Thomas by the hand, and seated himself by the bedside, saying, "My goodness, my boy, you look much better this morning. Are you ready for some news?"

Thomas's thoughts turned immediately to Gerda. "Is it good news?" he asked.

"Well," replied the chancellor, "here is some good news. The two men who held you to ransom were captured, tried and imprisoned. But the smaller one escaped, and tried to rob the goldsmith's house. But luckily I had put one of my men on guard, so he did not succeed."

"So where is he now? And where is my ring?" asked Thomas.

"The robber had a stolen horse, and he rode off into the forest. I do not think we shall ever see him again. As for your ring, it is here." The chancellor took the snake-ring from his purse, and held it up to the light, so that the gold and jewels sparkled. "Exquisite!" he said, "I wish it were mine. But it is yours; take it, and may you never lose it again."

As Thomas gratefully took the ring and thanked the chancellor, his thoughts turned once more to Gerda. His face clouded. "Is there any other news?" he asked.

The chancellor looked serious. "There are two young people waiting downstairs, who have news for you. But from what I hear, it seems that they are soon to be married. Their names are Gerda and Robert." Seeing the look of despair that crossed Thomas's face, he continued, "My boy, you will suffer for a while, but you are young, and time will heal your pain. And remember that the king's offer still holds good. There is always a place for you in the Shining Kingdom." He rose to leave. "I will see you again before I return to the king."

A few moments later Robert and Gerda entered the room. As soon as she caught sight of Thomas, Gerda rushed towards him, flung her arms around his neck, and gave him a long and loving kiss – and then burst into tears.

"Oh, Thomas, how can I tell you?" she sobbed.

"You are trying to tell me that you are going to marry Robert," said Thomas quietly.

"No, no, not that," cried Gerda, "it's about the ring. You will never forgive me. I lost the ring!"

Thomas took out the ring, and held it on the palm of

his hand for her to see. Gerda was so amazed that she stopped sobbing. Thomas thought she looked even more beautiful than he remembered, even with the tears streaming down her face.

Now Robert spoke. He was still the quiet, serious young man that Thomas remembered.

"Gerda and I agreed to be married at Easter, if you had not returned by then. We did this to please my parents, and so that we could both live in the farmhouse together. But now you are here, everything has changed. Gerda has never loved anyone but you, and so it is you two who will be married. All the arrangements are made, and the wedding will take place as arranged, but with you as bridegroom. Do you agree?"

"With all my heart," replied Thomas. "But what about you?" he asked, turning to Gerda.

"My heart has been yours since we worked together on the farm," she replied. "Of course I agree."

"What will you do?" Thomas asked Robert.

"My future is clear," he replied. "During the time you have been away, I have felt a call to become a priest. Now you are here to take care of Gerda, I am free to follow my calling. I shall make arrangements to enter a seminary, and from then on I must go wherever the Church decides to send me. And now I shall leave you two together, to tell each other your stories, and make up for the years when you have been apart."

Robert embraced them warmly, and took his leave.

CHAPTER 19

DANGER AT THE WEDDING

The wedding was to take place in the village church, which had been decorated with great bunches of primroses and daffodils. All the village had been invited, and there was to be a feast on the village green afterwards, with food and drink for all the guests.

The chancellor had insisted on putting off his return to the king's palace so that he could attend, and he had arranged for his soldiers to form a triumphal arch with their swords as the newly married couple left the church.

The day arrived, and it was a most beautiful spring day. Everyone said it would be the most wonderful wedding of the year. By now the story of Thomas's good fortune had spread far and wide, and all the villagers agreed that never before had a village girl married a prince. Everyone knew that the church would be full to overflowing, and that many people would have to wait outside to greet the newly married pair as they came out of the church.

The group of soldiers had arrived early and practised forming the archway quickly and neatly, and were now resting at the foot of a huge oak tree. This ancient oak spread its branches to within a hand's breadth of the church wall.

★ ★ ★

Zwerg had arrived at the church long before even the soldiers. Since he had fled from the town nothing had gone right for him. Without the help of Riese he did not dare to waylay travellers. He had several times ventured into the town after dark and stolen small amounts of money, but since the trial everyone was on the look out for him. When trying to buy food he was recognised and chased by groups of angry townspeople, and it was only because he was so slim and athletic that he managed to escape.

He blamed the snake-ring for his bad luck. "Ever since that Thomas brought his ring into our den, we have had a curse on us," he said to himself.

So he vowed to get his revenge on Thomas. *If he dies*, thought Zwerg, *they will bury the ring with him, and our ill-luck will be over*. When Zwerg heard about the wedding, he decided to spy out the church and its surroundings. He did this one moonlight night, and a plan came into his head.

Soon after dawn on the wedding morning Zwerg arrived at the church. He climbed the oak tree until he reached a branch, which almost touched the church wall. Above the porch there was a small window without glass. Once again Zwerg's small size and fitness came to his aid. He slid along the branch, squeezed through the window, and lay on one of the cross-beams that held up the church roof.

He had no weapon, so his plan was to take a large stone up to the high beam, and to drop it at the very moment when Thomas was passing underneath him. He had tried out the plan with small pebbles, and guessed quite correctly that Thomas and Gerda, once they were married, would walk slowly to the door, Gerda would be on Thomas's left. Zwerg was quite sure that he knew exactly when to release his stone, which in fact was a heavy, sharp piece of flint. He settled down to wait.

★ ★ ★

The church was packed with people. Many could not find room inside, and waited in the churchyard for the couple to come out. It was a wonderful scene. Thomas was dressed in his finery as Prince of the Shining Kingdom. Gerda was wearing her long, white wedding dress, that she had sat and sewed during many long nights of waiting. And there was Father Paulus, in his white Easter vestments, reciting in his deep, sincere voice the words that would join the two young people in marriage.

"I now pronounce you man and wife together."

The snake-ring on Gerda's slender finger had now been joined by a plain gold wedding ring. She looked into Thomas's face and smiled happily as they began their slow walk to the church door.

But before they could reach there, Gerda felt a sudden sharp pain in her ring finger, and a tingling like an electric shock ran up her arm. She stopped, catching her breath, and with a cry clung more tightly to Thomas's arm. Thomas stopped, and turned to her to ask what was wrong, and as he did so, a large jagged piece of flint dropped just in front of him, and split in two on the church paving.

Zwerg saw that his plan had failed but had not time to wait if he were going to escape. In a flash he moved along the beam, squeezed out of the small window, along the branch and down the tree – right into the arms of a burly soldier, one of the squad waiting to make an archway with their swords. By the time the newly-weds had been taken in their carriage to the village green to begin the great feast that had been prepared, Zwerg was safely back in prison.

CHAPTER 20

HAPPY EVER AFTER?

A platform had been built at one side of the green, and the crowds cheered as Thomas and Gerda climbed the steps. Thomas made a sign for the crowd to be silent, and then spoke to them:

"My friends," he said, "it would take too long to tell you of all the places I have been since I left the farm. But I have seen the world, and made my fortune. I have been greatly honoured by the king. But I have also been a prisoner, I have been poor and I have been hungry. I have lived in the king's palace and in a robbers' den. But now I am married, and I have come home.

"In all my travels, I was never as happy as when I was working with my sweetheart Gerda, on the farm. So that is what I will do. Tomorrow, I shall put on my working clothes and begin work on the farm. But once a year, on this day, I shall put on these fine clothes, and ride through the village and through the town and you will all remember who I am. All robbers and cheats and criminals of all kinds, keep away! Because I can bring the king's anger down upon you. So this land will be happy and peaceful, now and forever.

"And now, my friends, let the rejoicing begin! There is food and drink for all, and there will be singing and dancing far into the night!"

With that, amid more cheering from the crowds, Thomas and Gerda returned to their carriage, and were driven back to the farm, to be together as man and wife for the first time.

Thomas carried out his promise, and the story was told round many firesides in the land: of the farm-boy who became a prince, and then chose to be a farmer again, and the village girl who married the prince without the help of a fairy godmother.

Wilhelm and Gertrud lived to a ripe and comfortable old age, and Thomas made sure that they had every comfort in their cosy cottage.

Robert went to Spain to train as a priest, and when he was given a parish of his own, became a wise and holy counsellor to all the people.

But not everyone lived happily ever after. The king agreed that Thomas should be allowed to choose what punishment Riese and Zwerg should receive. He decided that he did not wish to see them hanged.

"After all," he explained to the chief magistrate, "they could have treated me much worse when I was their prisoner. They shall be sent under armed guard to the king's palace. Each winter Riese will keep every room in the palace supplied with coal and logs for the fires. All through the summer, he will cut wood and saw logs for the winter. There are nearly two hundred rooms in the palace.

"Zwerg will spend his time cleaning out the king's stables. There are over a hundred horses. If either of them tries to escape, then they will be kept in a dark cell without windows."

"Of course, the king could pardon them at any time, but I do not think he will."

And so the story draws to its end. But if you were to visit the farm by the two rivers at haymaking time, you would see two happy people working in the hayfield. If you were to look closely you would see that the girl is wearing a wedding ring and also another ring: a most unusual one formed from two snakes intertwined, with jewels for eyes. And if you were to listen, you might hear two melodious voices singing together:

I mow by the Neckar, I mow by the Rhine,
And now I'm so happy, my sweetheart is mine.

If you have enjoyed the story, perhaps you would like to know where the idea for it came from.

'Des Knaben Wunderhorn' (The Boy's Magic Horn) is a collection of old German folk poems. One of these, called 'A Little Rhine Legend' tells the story of how a girl loses her ring in the river, and how it appears on the king's table.

However, I have invented the characters, and the story of how it all happened.

John Holroyd
2003